# *Good Enough*
## *and Other Stories*

Rachel Vail

Jack Gantos

Susan Shreve

**SCHOLASTIC INC.**
New York  Toronto  London  Auckland  Sydney
Mexico City  New Delhi  Hong Kong

## Cover and interior illustrations by
## Kris Dresen

# *Contents*

# Good Enough

I stood on the toilet lid, staring into the bathroom mirror. Then I flushed the toilet with my foot, so my brothers—and especially my mother—wouldn't suspect anything. I jumped down from the toilet and turned on the hot water full blast. I soaked my washcloth in the steaming water until my palms burned, then pressed it quickly onto my face. I breathed in, through the wet heat. After I dried my face on the damp hand towel, I took one more deep breath and attempted a smile.

I hoped nobody could tell I'd been crying.

Mom gasped happily when I stepped out of the bathroom. "Oh, it fits perfectly! Boys,

took at Dori!" She pulled me out to the deck and I twirled around, not trusting myself to speak, as my brothers complimented me in my new shirt. "Cute, Dori." "Looks good." I looked up at my dad, who was sunk into his chair, watching. "You look beautiful, sweetheart," he said.

I tried to say thank you, but only the "thank" came out. I pressed my lips together and counted to 210 by 7s—although math is what got me into this mess in the first place.

My troubles started a few days ago. My mom had come home between shifts working at the diner. I was busy with my math homework. She sat down next to me, and put her swollen feet up on the kitchen table. Mom tries to come home between shifts whenever she can, even though my older brothers are supposed to be around to watch me and Nate. I am really old enough to keep myself out of trouble. I just do homework or read. I have never in my whole life caused trouble, anyway. Well, until now. And this trouble is just for myself.

"So, have you thought of what you want for your birthday yet?" I remember Mom asking. I rested my forehead in the space between my thumb and my index finger, leaning in closer to the math problem I was figuring out.

"Come on," she urged, after a gulp of her iced tea. "I gotta get back to work. What are you really hoping for?"

"An Orion shirt," I mumbled, still trying to focus on my math. It was the first week of school, and it's important to me to make a good start, not fall behind.

"What's an Orion shirt?" Mom asked enthusiastically. I shook my head. I hadn't meant to say anything. I erased the column of numbers I'd been working on.

"Tell me," Mom said, giving me a nudge with her iced-tea glass. "What's an Orion shirt? I never heard of that. Don't chew on your lips, Dori, they get so chapped."

I let my lip slip out of my teeth and said quietly, "It's nothing, just a kind of shirt."

"That everybody wears?"

I shrugged, then nodded, but dusted my eraser crumbs away instead of looking at her. "They're just, you know, soft cotton, like knit. With a collar. And on the left collar there are three little black stars."

"Oh, yeah," Mom said cheerfully. "I've seen a lot of the girls wearing those at the diner. They're the 'thing' this year?"

I shrugged. "But they're expensive."

"Oh." Mom stood up and kissed me on the top of my head. "Well, maybe the strike will end soon."

"Maybe," I said. My father's union had been on strike since July, more than two months already. Every day my mother told me maybe it would end soon. We hadn't even gone shopping for school supplies, our annual family tradition the weekend before school starts. I was still using last year's notebook, trying to concentrate on writing small, not using too much paper.

"I don't *really* want an Orion shirt," I told her as she rinsed her iced-tea glass. "I was just kidding. What I'd really like is, um, maybe a package of colored pencils. You know, the eight pack, like in AJ's store." I knew my brother AJ could get them for a 40 percent discount at the stationery store where he works after school.

"We'll see," Mom said, leaving. "I better hustle."

The only reason the Orion shirt had ever even entered my mind at all was that Lisa

Verilli has the locker next to mine again this year. Every morning I hear her and Carleen and their other friends complimenting each other—on their Orion shirts, and on their hair, their homework, their ice skating, their singing, everything.

They are polite girls, and pretty, never really outwardly mean, at least not to me. Lisa even whispers "Hi" to me sometimes. She gave me a half a hug the first day of school this year. But mostly she doesn't notice me; none of them do.

They are the A-group, the most popular girls in school. I am in no group at all. I do my work and I go home. Although they are as polite with one another as grown-up ladies, the A-group scares me a little.

The day when Mom was asking me what I wanted for my birthday, Lisa and Carleen and the others in the A-group had been comparing which colors of Orion shirts they had gotten to start the school year. Yellow and white seemed to be the top two, though I wasn't paying really close attention. But as I closed

my locker, I turned my head and found myself eye to eye with Lisa.

She flicked her eyes down my body, taking in the hand-me-down T-shirt with the faded football on it, from my brother Cal, and the brown corduroy shorts gathered up by a belt AJ had grown out of.

She smiled sympathetically, which is what

made me feel bad. I shrugged, to show I don't care about surface things like what I wear, and walked away.

But later, when I was at the kitchen table with my mother and her iced tea, I was thinking about myself in an Orion shirt. I was imagining how it would feel to get one of those purring compliments: *"Oh, Dori! That's the exact Orion shirt I wanted! But it looks much better on you."*

I was fantasizing what it might feel like, to look good enough.

The night of my birthday, we cooked out in the backyard—hot dogs, my favorite, and a white cake with chocolate frosting. My little brother, Nate, whispered to me, "And there is a big, beautiful present with a card with a rainbow on it, but don't tell anybody because it's a secret." I promised I wouldn't tell anybody, but he was so excited he couldn't even eat his cake; so Mom let him give me the presents. There were two, held together with a yellow ribbon.

On top was a card drawn by Nate, a picture

of a girl with long, long hair, much longer than mine, standing beneath a rainbow. On the inside it said, "DORI—HPPY BDAY. U R THE B." That's Nate's way of writing you are the best. He's only 4 1/2.

I let him tear open the small wrapped box. It was a box of colored pencils, the eight pack. I hugged them and said thanks, and wondered for a second what the big box could be, until I realized. I tore open the wrapping paper, and saw that in that box was a shirt. A soft, knit shirt with a collar. And on the left collar, three little black...hearts.

My stomach dropped. It was a fake Orion, a cheap imitation, with hearts instead of stars. It was still too expensive, probably, for my mother to be buying for me this year. And it was worse than no Orion shirt at all. It was the fakeness that was so awful. I'd rather wear my brothers' old T-shirts. At least they are what they are, and don't try to be anything else.

I held up the fake shirt for everybody to see, while my mother explained that it was an

Orion shirt, the hottest trend of the year for the girls in my class. I chewed on my lip and she didn't stop me. I gave her and my dad kisses, thanked them for the presents, and quickly helped clean up all the wrapping and paper plates so I wouldn't have to look at anybody. But when I got back outside, there was Mom, holding up the shirt, saying, "Go try it on, Dori. Let's see how it looks!"

So I went obediently to the bathroom, tried it on, cried at my reflection, modeled it for the family, then headed straight for my room. I peeled it off and put on a comfortable old pair of pajamas. I folded the shirt and placed it neatly in my drawer, and closed the drawer tight. When Mom said I should come watch TV with everybody, I yelled down that I was tired and had to finish reading a book for school the next day.

Mom came up. "Hey, birthday girl," she said. I kept reading, while she laid out my clothes for the morning: my brown corduroys and belt, and the imitation Orion.

I opened my mouth to protest, but no words came. Just shame. Shame at not being able to afford the real thing, a rehearsal shame for the real shame I knew I'd feel when Lisa and Carleen and the others in the A-group saw me the next morning at the lockers.

I could see myself standing there wearing a fake, a *wish-I-had-what-you-have-but-I-can't-*

*afford-it* imitation wrong shirt. Not good enough. I turned away while my mother tucked the blanket tight around me. "You are so loved," she whispered.

At the lockers early in the morning, Lisa looked at me, not unkindly. But then Carleen yanked on her yellow Orion sleeve and whispered in her ear. I hung onto my locker and waited. I tasted the salty tear that had slipped out by accident. I raised my eyes to meet Lisa's.

"New shirt?" she asked.

I nodded, and another tear fell, this one plunking straight down onto my arm.

Carleen taunted, "Is it an Orion?"

I shook my head and kept on crying, ready for the humiliation and punishment I knew I deserved. "No," I blubbered, ashamed, "it's a fake."

Then I blinked, and the tears stopped. I just suddenly couldn't believe that I, of all people, would be standing in the middle of school, crying about my shirt. These tears are what I should be ashamed of, I realized—not the shirt, not the hearts instead of stars.

The eyebrows of the A-group were all raised. I touched the bottom hem of my new shirt. It felt very soft. I imagined my mother standing at the display at the Price Club. I pictured her rubbing the material, adding up how much it would cost with tax, how much it would subtract from how little we had. Then I imagined her picking up the shirt anyway to carry it proudly to the checkout for her daughter. *You are so loved*, I heard inside my head.

A fake? Depends what's real, I guess. I smiled at the A-group and told them, "But it's the best present I ever got."

I walked away feeling good enough.

Why does Dori say that the shirt is the best present she ever got?

# The Penny Tree

"What are you getting Pete for his birthday?" my older sister, Betsy, asked. Pete was my younger brother. He was going to be five years old and I hadn't gotten him a thing.

"I'm still thinking about it," I answered as I wedged my hand between the couch cushions.

"You are not *thinking*," Betsy shot back. "You are couch-fishing for change because you're broke."

"I've got plenty of cash," I replied, lying as my fingers desperately clawed the mysterious spaces within the couch.

"You spend all your money on yourself," she said, reading my mind. I had just spent

most of my cash on a Mo Vaughn baseball card.

"Ah ha!" I shouted, and pulled an old penny out of the crack. "Now I've got something for Pete." I held the penny up for her to see. "This little penny will change his life," I announced, without the slightest idea how it might do so. But I kept talking. "You don't need a lot of cash to give a great gift." I rapped my knuckles against my head. "You just need a generous imagination."

"That's just another way of saying you are cheap!" she said, sneering.

"Just you wait," I snapped back. "With this one penny I will steal the birthday gift-giving show."

"Put your money where your mouth is," she said. "I bet ten bucks—that's a thousand pennies—that my gift will be his favorite."

"You're on," I replied, thinking that I did need a "generous imagination." Quick.

I grabbed the classified section of the newspaper off the coffee table and went into my bedroom. What can I buy for a penny, I wondered, as I stared at the ads. Cars were too expensive. I turned the page. Houses, furniture, and exotic pets were out of my price range. There was nothing for a penny at the grocery store, shoe store, toy store, bookstore—any store. In fact, nothing in Miami could be bought for a penny. Why do they even make them? I asked myself. They just end up behind couch cushions, in jars, jammed into penny loafers, lost under refrigerators, sucked into vacuum cleaners, or swallowed by crawling babies. They certainly were a lot more trouble than they were worth.

Buying something for a penny was definitely out of the question. I was back to where I started. But then I glanced at one more ad. A plant store was having a sale. Still, even a bag of dirt, which I could get for free in my back yard, cost two dollars. Even a jug of tap water was more than my budget could handle. Then suddenly my generous imagination saved the day.

After dinner Mom brought out a birthday cake. She lit the five candles and said to Pete, "Honey, make a wish."

Pete's eyes floated up toward the ceiling as he sucked a whole roomful of air into his lungs, then leaned forward. The five little flames didn't know what hit them. In a split second there was nothing left but five vanishing trails of smoke.

"Okay," Pete announced, grinning. "I'm ready to open presents."

Mom and Dad lifted a big box onto the table. Small trains crisscrossed the wrapping paper.

Pete ripped it open with one swipe and lifted the top on the box. There was a train set with a steam locomotive and lots of old-time cattle cars, and water tankers and a red caboose.

"Awesome!" Pete shrieked, and threw his arms around Mom and Dad. "Thank you," he said.

Mom and Dad spent a lot more than a penny, but I wasn't worried. My generous imagination had been extra generous.

Suddenly Pete turned toward Betsy. "Next," he said.

She gave him a big package with a huge bow on the top. Pete yanked the bow off, peeled the paper back, and flipped open the top of a box. He pulled out a pair of train engineer's striped bib overalls, a matching denim cap, and a red bandanna.

"You are the best sister on the planet," he said and gave her a hug. I figured she must have spent at least twenty bucks.

Then he looked at me. I felt my ears turn red. The heat was on. I supposed if I hadn't spent all my money on my card collection I would be giving him a pocket watch or a silver-plated

railroad spike or something that would fit the gift-giving theme. Still, I didn't lose faith in my generous imagination.

"So," Betsy cut in with her smarmy voice, "what did you get Pete?"

I reached into my shirt pocket and removed a small manila envelope. On the front of it I had drawn a tree covered with tiny pennies. Under the drawing I had written: One Penny Tree seed.

I handed it to him. He opened the metal clasp

and shook out the single penny and a piece of paper with "Planting Instructions." He looked suspiciously at the penny, then back at me. Then Mom and Dad and Betsy stared at me. They did not seem pleased with my choice of gifts.

I snatched the Planting Instructions out of his hand. "It reads, 'Plant in fertile soil and water six times daily until a penny tree grows.'"

"Will it actually grow?" he asked.

"Oh yeah," I shot back. "Absolutely. It's guaranteed. Says so right on the directions."

"Wow!" he shouted. "This is the best gift ever. When the tree grows I'll have enough pennies to buy an entire real train."

"Sure you will," I said with my generous imagination getting away from me. "You could even buy the old Santa Fe Railroad and ride it across the desert."

Then he ran out the back door to go plant his seed.

"Jack," Mom said, "I hope you haven't started something you will regret. Your brother believes everything you say, so don't you dare let him down."

"Don't worry," I said to Mom. "It's under control."

As soon as she was out of the room I turned to Betsy and stuck out my hand. "That will be one thousand pennies, please."

She gave me a jar of change and a few bills. "Mark my words. When you mess this up, this money is coming right back, plus another ten."

"We'll see," I replied.

The next morning Pete woke before me. When I got up I peeked out the kitchen window. There he was, watering his seed. I smiled to myself as I poured milk on my cereal. What an incredible gift, I thought. This was definitely the smartest thing I had ever cooked up. It only cost me one free cent, and on top of it I made a thousand more from Betsy. I felt like a genius. As I ate, I began to imagine what baseball card I'd buy next.

When Pete came in he was excited. "I think it is growing already," he said.

"Could be," I replied. "Just remember, water it six times per day or else it will shrivel up and die." I figured he'd never be able to keep up the six times per day schedule and sooner or later I'd have to announce the death of the penny tree. And I will be blameless. It was perfect.

But the first warning I had that Pete's generous imagination was bigger than mine was when he came running up to me holding the windup alarm clock in his outstretched hands.

"How many hours apart is it if I water six times per day?" he asked.

I did the math in my head. "Four," I replied.

"Then set this for four hours from now," he said.

I did. When I handed it back to him he grabbed his little red plastic play chair and went outside. When I looked out the window again he was sitting in his chair, reading a book with the alarm clock on his lap and the watering can to his side. Cute, I thought. Very cute. I should take a picture.

"Where's Pete?" Mom asked. "We have to go to the store and get more train track."

"Out back," I said, and pointed toward the window.

She looked out. "Oh, that is precious," she said. But then her voice grew serious. "Jack, you know your brother still believes in Santa Claus, the Easter Bunny, and the Tooth Fairy. It would be awful of you to burst his bubble."

"He's a little brother," I said. "It's a law that older brothers have to burst the bubbles of little brothers."

"Just don't hurt him," she warned me. "Or there is a parent's law that says there might be consequences."

That was her favorite warning, "There might be consequences." This always got my generous imagination worked up. Usually I pictured myself wrapped in chains and handcuffed to a post in our spider-filled attic.

That night the alarm went off at midnight, and again at four in the morning. Each time Pete hopped out of bed, turned on his flashlight, and ran outside to water his penny tree. Each time, I had to set the alarm for him.

By morning, I was beginning to feel the "consequences" creeping up on me.

All the next day Pete kept up his watering routine, and I kept my mouth shut. That night we were sitting in the living room reading. Pete pulled out his old copy of *The Carrot Seed*. He knew the story by heart and flipped through the pages over and over. "This is the greatest book ever!" he shouted. "The little boy plants a carrot seed and waters it and waters it and even though everyone in his family says it won't grow he still waters it because *he* believes it will. And then, *boom*, overnight it grows into a giant carrot. That's just how it is going to be with my penny tree because *I* believe in it!"

I peeked over the top of my book. Mom, Dad, and Betsy were peeking up over their books— and they were glaring at me. I smiled back. They didn't.

Suddenly, I was beginning to feel bad about myself. Maybe I had gone too far. Maybe Pete was too delicate for my scheme. "I'll be right back," I announced, and put my book down. I ran to the garage and got a garden spade. Then I went over to the neighbor's yard and dug up a plant that sort of looked like a little tree. Then I replanted it where Pete had planted his seed.

I sneaked back into my bedroom and got a handful of pennies and some tape, then went back outside. Quickly, I taped a few pennies on the branches. "This will make him happy," I said to myself, "and then we can forget about the penny tree."

The next morning Pete woke me up by jumping up and down on my bed and shouting. "It grew! It grew! I'm rich. Come see!"

I hopped up and followed him outside. "Wow," I said, and made my eyes get real big.

"It worked."

He bent down and held one in his hands. "Why are they held on with tape?" he asked.

"That's not tape," I said. "Those are penny stems."

"Cool," he said. Then he asked a question that I gave the wrong answer to. "If I leave them on the tree will they grow really big, like huge penny hubcaps?"

"Nah," I replied, "they'll turn into nickels."

Pete's eyes bugged out. "Nickels!" he shouted. "Then I'll wait to pick them."

Oh, no, I thought. I did it again.

Everything went downhill fast from there. And the more broke I became, the happier everyone else was. First, I had to sneak out in the middle of the night and change the pennies to nickels. And of course Pete was thrilled. When he saw them he danced a little dance around the yard and then announced that he would wait for them to become dimes. Once again, I dug into my piggy bank and got dimes and later sneaked out and put them on the tree. The following morning Pete went nuts. He did somersaults across the yard and drooled all over himself. Then he decided to hold out for quarters. That night, I changed the dimes to quarters. The next day Pete went screaming wildly around the backyard until he was so dizzy he fell over and announced he would wait for fifty-cent pieces. I had seen it coming, so I'd gotten Mom to exchange the money I'd won from Betsy for half dollars at the bank.

That night I did the changeover. The next day, he was bonkers. I tried to get him to pluck the half dollars off the tree, but no, he was holding out for the dollar bills. That night, I gave the half dollars back to Mom for singles. I taped ten bills all over the tree, and when I finished I said to myself, "Okay, I've broken even—this madness has got to stop. I started it, so I'll finish it."

I got a small pair of scissors and cut off all the leaves from the tree and left them scattered under the tiny branches.

The next morning Pete and I got up together to water the tree. On the way out of the house he said, "Maybe after the single-dollar bills there

will be five-dollar bills, then tens, then twenties, then hundreds . . ." I stopped him. "Don't count your chickens before they hatch," I warned him, sounding like my father.

When we arrived at the tree Pete gasped and dropped to his knees. "It died!" he shouted. "All its leaves fell off." He began to cry.

"But dollar bills are still left on the bare branches," I pointed out.

"Why'd it die?" he blubbered. "I loved this tree."

"It's not dead," I said, putting my arm around his shoulders. "It's just that winter is coming. The penny tree has a short growing season. You know, like oranges and limes."

Pete wiped his eyes on his sleeve. Then he thought about what I'd said. He thought about it for so long that I knew I was in trouble.

"You mean it will return next summer?" he asked.

"Yes," I said. "Of course it will."

"That is so cool!" he shouted. "I'll be rich all over again."

He was ripping the dollar bills off the tree as I stood up and slowly walked back to my room. I shook my piggy bank. It was empty. I better start saving now, I thought. That kid's generous imagination is going to cost me every red cent I can get my hands on.

How do you think Jack feels about his little brother, Pete?

# V.W. and Me

I have always been in trouble at Stockton Elementary in Stockton, New Jersey. Ever since first grade, when Ms. Percival sent me home early on Halloween for stuffing Mary Sue Briggs's lavender teddy bear into the lower-school toilet.

"It's not that you're bad, Benjamin," my mother would tell me when I was younger. "You just have a bad reputation because of the teddy bear."

Nevertheless, my report card used to read like a prison record. Full of U's for Unsatisfactory, and D's for Disrespectful, Disturbing, Difficult, Disorganized, Dumb, Dreadful, Disgusting.

And long paragraphs of recommendations for my improvement, and the suggestion that I might be happier in a private school.

"Honestly, Ben," my father said at the end of fourth grade, "you've *got* to pull yourself together, or we'll be visiting you at the juvenile detention home."

And then this year, fifth grade with Mr. Baker, something changed.

My report cards sparkled with good news. I was smart in class and good at soccer and quiet during library. I helped out on the playground, tutored some third-graders in reading, got a speaking part in the school play, and was elected to be on traffic patrol. Even the music teacher, who last year recommended that I spend music periods in the principal's office, told me I had a remarkable singing voice.

"What happened?" my father asked.

"I don't know," I shrugged. "All of a sudden, I'm a different person."

"You're the same person," my mother said in her reasonable voice. "Just acting different."

And then V.W. arrived at Stockton

Elementary, the week after Easter break. Fifth grade. Mr. Baker. Just my luck. He took a quick look around the classroom considering the possibilities for a friend, and decided on me. And that was that. When the bell rang for the end of homeroom, he jumped up from his chair, rushed over three rows to where I was sitting, and attached himself like Velcro to my side.

V.W. Sanger was tall, almost as tall as my father, and skinny, with soft, yellow hair that hung below his ears, and glasses, and a deep dimple in his chin. I wouldn't have even noticed the dimple if he hadn't drawn a question mark in the middle of it with red Magic Marker.

"I hate this school," he said to me after first period when I was walking with him to the library to meet Ms. Bissell. "I could tell the minute I arrived this morning. It has a kind of bad smell."

I sniffed. It smelted like a perfectly ordinary school to me, the same as it always smelled.

"So?" V.W. said after we left the library. "I

suppose you're wondering where I got the question mark on my chin."

Of course I was wondering. It looked like a bright-red sunburn, or an infected mosquito bite. Or a large zit.

"I always draw a question mark on my chin in every school I go to, and I've been to seven schools in five years," he said. "I suppose you're wondering what it means."

I nodded, although I hadn't even gotten around to wondering what it meant.

"It means, 'Who knows what's going to happen with me around?' I'm a big question mark." He gave my shoulder a little shove. "Get it?"

"Right," I said. "I get it."

The first day he walked with me to every class—first music, then library and gym and lunch and computer and Spanish. Wherever he went, he sat right next to me, slid halfway down in his chair so it looked as if he was going to fall on the floor, and looked at the teacher through half-closed lizard eyes.

"So," each teacher would begin at the start of class. "You're V.W."

"Right," V.W. would say.

"And where are you from?"

"Chicago," V.W. said in music. "Minneapolis," he said in library. "San Francisco," he said in gym. "Miami," he said in computer. No one contradicted him, but by the time we got to Spanish, where he said he was from China, we were struggling not to laugh.

"How come you change where you're

from?" I asked at the end of the school day.

"I get bored easily," V.W. said.

I don't know why I used to cause so much trouble in school. It just happened. But my mother said things don't just happen, and my father added that I was responsible for making them happen, and my sister Rosie said that I caused trouble in school because I was uncomfortable.

Sometimes I think about the word "uncomfortable" because Rosie was right about me. Uncomfortable is like having on the wrong clothes or thinking everyone is looking at you or whispering behind your back. Or maybe you have sprouts growing out of the top of your head. Whatever, it's a terrible way to feel and it made me do bad things.

The thing I haven't said is that I talk funny. I have a lisp, which means that my tongue gets stuck between my teeth when I say words with *S* in them. So instead of saying, "May I please have a bowl of soup," I say, "May I pleath have a bowl of thoup."

Thoup was the reason I put Mary Sue's stupid teddy bear in the toilet. We were sitting in the lunchroom at the beginning of first grade, Mary Sue on one side of me and Billy Bass on the other, and Billy said to me, "What did you bring in your thermos?"

"Tomato thoup," I said.

"Tomato thoup?" Mary Sue asked. "I never heard of that."

"He means soup," Billy said.

"But he said *thoup*," Mary Sue said and she turned to Etty Suregate on the other side of her and said, "Did you hear that Ben has tomato *thoup* in his thermos?" and she fell off her chair laughing.

"Say my name," she said, when she could control herself.

"Rat fink," I said, since I certainty wasn't going to say Mary Thoo.

I got up from the table, thinking that I'd be perfectly happy to pour my tomato soup over her curly brown hair. But I didn't. Instead I went back to the classroom, took her lavender teddy bear out of her cubby, and went into the

bathroom for first-and second-graders. Ms. Percival found me stuffing the bear's head into the hole at the bottom of the toilet.

After that, I felt uncomfortable all the time. I didn't want to read aloud in class. I thought in advance of everything I was going to say, worried that someone would make fun of me if I lisped. I had a fluttery feeling in my stomach every day I walked up the front steps of the school.

Besides, since the teddy bear problem, everyone expected trouble from me.

So that's what they got, until this year. I don't know exactly what made me change. Maybe I just got sort of sick of getting in trouble. So I stopped doing things that got me into trouble. And then another thing happened. I started doing good things, and I liked how it felt. I liked it when I studied hard for a math test and got 100 and my mom hung the test on the fridge. I liked it when I put away all the balls at recess without anyone asking, and my gym teacher shouted, "Thanks a lot, Benjamin!" in front of everyone. My mom sent me to a new speech therapist and my lisp started to go away. I didn't feel so uncomfortable anymore.

So now, what do I do about this creep with a question mark on his chin? He's stuck to me like flypaper, and I don't really want people to notice that.

"So, we're friends, right?" V.W. asked, at the beginning of his second day of school, standing at the top of the steps of Stockton Elementary. "Real friends, right?"

"Right," I said without much enthusiasm.

This morning the question mark in the dimple on his chin was blue Magic Marker with a yellow dot. I decided to pretend I hadn't seen it.

In homeroom, Mr. Baker asked V.W. about his last school.

"I went to three schools last year," V.W. said. "One in New Jersey, one in Connecticut, and one in Pensacola, Florida. My father changes jobs all the time." This time I could tell he was being honest.

"That's a lot of schools," Mr. Baker said, looking hard at the question mark on V.W.'s chin. I guess he was considering whether to ask him to wash it off and decided not to. "Well, I hope you like Stockton."

"I don't think the kids in this stupid school like me," V.W. said to me when the bell rang for first-period math.

"How come?" I asked. "They don't even

know you yet."

"I can tell," V.W. said. "You can always tell the way kids are sort of looking at you like you're some kind of freak."

"The kids here are pretty nice," I said, getting my math book out of my locker. But I knew what he meant of course, since that was the way I had felt until this year.

"Maybe you ought to stop wearing that question mark," I said. I thought about it before I told V.W. about the question mark, knowing that I don't like kids to tell me what to do. But I was feeling kind of bad for him and thinking maybe I could help him out if he was uncomfortable like I had been.

Instead, he looked at me with this strange expression, as if I had lost my mind.

"If I didn't have a question mark on my chin, I'd be invisible," he said, and his voice was full of tears. "No one would even know I was here."

That night, lying in bed after my lights were out, listening to my parents in the kitchen scrubbing the pots while they talked about the day, I thought about what V.W. had said.

"What does it mean when someone says they're invisible?" I asked my mother when she came into the bedroom to kiss me good night.

Mom thought for a minute. "I guess that nobody notices them, or cares about them. Do you feel invisible, sweetheart?"

"Not me," I said. "This new boy called V.W. does. Already he's been to three schools this year."

"Poor V.W.", my mother said. "Of course he feels invisible. Who wouldn't?"

When I finally fell asleep that night, I was thinking about poor V.W. and all those schools and new friends and teachers and houses. I'm the kind of boy who hates change, even the end of school or the end of summer or the end of Christmas vacation.

The next morning when I arrived at Stockton, V.W. was in trouble. He was sitting outside the principal's office, the bill of a baseball cap pulled down over half his face, an

orange question mark on his chin, his hands in his lap.

I slid on the couch next to him.

"What's up?" I asked.

"I hate this school."

"I know," I said. "I used to hate it too."

"Yeah?" V.W lifted his baseball cap. "How come?"

"I lisped," I said. "I used to lisp a lot and kids made fun of me."

"And what did you do?"

"Got in trouble. All the time I used to be in trouble."

"Me, too," V.W. said. "Every time I get to a new school, I get in trouble."

"What did you do today?" I asked.

"I wrote "BABY" on Mary Sue Briggs's math book yesterday because she called me a "pretty girl," and she told the principal, and the principal told me to wait here because he had a lot to talk to me about."

I began to laugh.

And I told him about first grade and Mary Sue and the lavender teddy bear.

"Maybe it's Mary Sue who should be waiting to talk to the principal," I suggested.

V.W. cracked a smile.

"So show me your lisp," he said.

"V.W. Thanger," I said.

"My name is V.W. *Sanger*," he said, smiling.

"That's what I thaid." I threw my arm around his shoulder. V.W. Thanger."

The principal opened the door to his office and motioned for V.W. to come in.

"I'm coming, too," I said.

"You, Ben?" the principal asked. "How come?"

"I thought maybe I could help," I said, picking up my backpack and walking into the office. "V.W. is my good friend."

Would you want Ben for a friend? Why or why not?